SPACE SCOUT

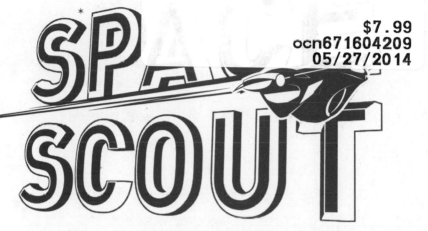

SCOUTING THE UNIVERSE FOR A NEW EARTH

The Kid Kingdom
published in 2011 by
Hardie Grant Egmont
85 High Street
Prahran, Victoria 3181, Australia
www.hardiegrantegmont.com.au

A CiP record for this title is available from the National Library of Australia

Text copyright © 2011 H. Badger
Illustration and design copyright © 2011 Hardie Grant Egmont

Cover illustration by M. Deeble
Illustrated by D. Greulich
Series design by S. Swingler
Typeset by Ektavo
Printed in Australia by McPherson's Printing Group

1 3 5 7 9 10 8 6 4 2

SPACE SCOUT™

THE KID KINGDOM

BY **H. BADGER**

ILLUSTRATED BY **D. GREULICH**

hardie grant EGMONT

CHAPTER 1

Kip Kirby was puffed. He was trying to put up a volleyball net. It wasn't easy, because Kip kept floating into the air. So did the net!

Not surprising, Kip grinned to himself. *I* am *on the moon.*

Kip and his best friend Jett were camping with their dads. It was the year 2354 and the moon was a popular weekend getaway spot. It was too crowded on Earth to go camping.

Kip and Jett were excited about playing lunar volleyball. The low gravity on the moon made it perfect for awesome jump serves and spikes!

Kip's dad was unpacking the camping gear, kicking up gigantic clouds of lunar dust. 'How do you know when the moon's angry, boys?' he asked.

Kip and Jett shrugged their shoulders.

'It shows you its dark side!' Kip's dad chuckled.

Underneath his space helmet, Kip rolled his eyes. *How did I end up with such an embarrassing dad?* he thought.

Kip's image was especially important because he had a job as a Space Scout. Space Scouts explored distant galaxies to find a new planet to live on. There were so many people on Earth that they needed more room.

At 12 years old, Kip was the youngest of the 50 Space Scouts.

Kip loved his job. How many other kids had seen the awesome stuff he had on his missions?

'Coming at you, Kip!' Jett yelled.

Kip kept his eyes on the volleyball, which was floating over the net towards him.

'Got it,' Kip replied, leaping three

metres into the air to lob the volleyball back to Jett.

'Not the volleyball!' Jett yelled. 'THAT THING OVER THERE!'

Kip turned to see a black football-sized capsule hurtling towards him.

Red-hot flames spewed from the back of the capsule, which was fitted with powerful mini-rockets. Splashed on the side in big letters were the words:

With a second to spare, Kip ducked out of the way. His spacesuit was made from the latest ultra-light heat-resistant fabric, of course. But a sizzling hot capsule could still put a hole in it.

SMACK!

With a sickening crack, the capsule smashed into the moon's rocky surface. It broke open on impact and a wireless device floated out. It beamed encrypted data to Kip's SpaceCuff in seconds, and the SpaceCuff automatically decoded it.

A SpaceCuff was a communication device, translator and gaming console all rolled into one. Space Scouts would be lost without them.

MESSAGE FROM WORLDCORP

Go immediately to the Intergalactic Hoverport. You're needed on your next mission.

Incoming message

'Cool!' said Jett, who had read the message over Kip's shoulder. 'Where are they sending you?'

'I don't know,' said Kip. 'But I can't wait to find out! The only thing is…how do I get to the Hoverport?'

The Hoverport was 10 kilometres above Earth – a quick trip by Space Scout standards. But getting there from the moon was trickier.

Kip glanced around for inspiration. His eyes settled on his dad's brand-new Space Stream flying motor home.

The Space Stream was sleek, silver and decked out with extras like multi-galaxy cable TV and a rooftop waterless spa.

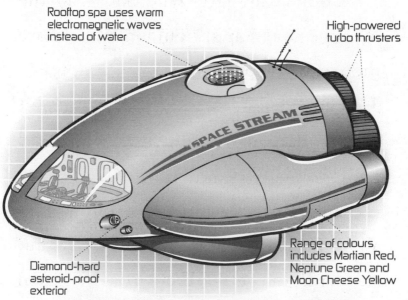

Rooftop spa uses warm electromagnetic waves instead of water

High-powered turbo thrusters

Diamond-hard asteroid-proof exterior

Range of colours includes Martian Red, Neptune Green and Moon Cheese Yellow

Space Stream Motor Home

Kip's dad never, *ever* let anyone fly it but him.

'You're not thinking what I think you're thinking, are you, Kip?' whispered Jett.

'I'd just be borrowing it,' Kip hissed back. 'As soon as I get to the Hoverport, I'll send it back here on auto-pilot. You guys can fly home to Earth, no problems.'

'Your dad's going to *kill* you!' Jett said, shaking his head.

Kip shrugged, but inside he was grinning. Secretly, he'd always wanted an excuse to fly the Space Stream.

Kip looked over at his dad, who was staring at their camping gear, bewildered.

Even though the Space Stream had the latest vertical hammocks, Kip's dad insisted on sleeping in the great outdoors. Otherwise, he said, it just wasn't a proper camping trip!

Instead of tents, moon campers needed

special inflatable structures with built-in airlocks. They were *supposed* to pop up in one go. But Kip's dad was having trouble with the instructions.

Now's my chance! Kip thought.

He felt a little guilty about sneaking off. At home, Kip had to do what his parents said, like any kid. It was only on Space Scout missions that he had complete control.

Kip's dad might be angry about the Space Stream at first. But Kip hoped he'd understand. He had to get to the Hoverport somehow. Earth's future could depend on Kip's next mission!

With a goodbye wave to Jett, Kip sneaked aboard the Space Stream. It was docked a little way from the campsite.

He jumped straight into the cockpit and commenced launch sequence.

As an experienced Space Scout, Kip was confident flying most vehicles. Besides, he'd watched his dad piloting the Space Stream heaps of times before.

With the roar of rockets powering up, the Space Stream took off into the air.

Through the windscreen, Kip saw his dad look up from the camping gear. His expression quickly went from surprised to mega-cranky.

'I'll look after it, Dad,' Kip called. 'Space Scout's honour!'

The Space Stream's powerful engine

throbbed as Kip hit the throttle. He understood why his dad loved flying it! It wasn't long before Kip left the moon far behind. And only a short time later, he arrived at the Intergalactic Hoverport.

All intergalactic space flights left from the Hoverport. That's why Kip's starship, MoNa 4000, was docked there. MoNa was a huge, glossy black ship, with a pointed nose cone and extra noisy thrusters, specially designed for extreme long-distance space travel. She was the ideal starship, apart from her bossy personality.

Kip expertly piloted the Space Stream into the massive landing bay on MoNa's lowest level.

MoNa had a team of maintenance robots aboard. Straight away, the bots began refuelling the Space Stream so it could return itself to the moon.

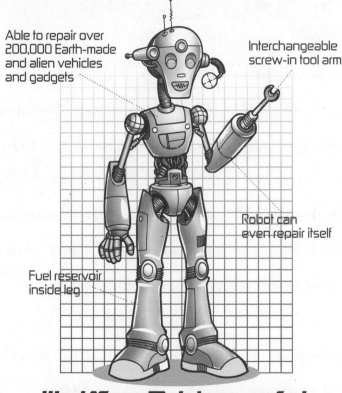

Able to repair over 200,000 Earth-made and alien vehicles and gadgets

Interchangeable screw-in tool arm

Robot can even repair itself

Fuel reservoir inside leg

WorldCorp Maintenancebot

Kip punched the co-ordinates for the moon into the Space Stream's control panel, then leapt out.

The Space Stream took off and MoNa's voice came over the loudspeaker. 'Airlock closed. Now stop wasting time and get to the bridge.'

Kip raced to MoNa's command centre, where a familiar furry figure was waiting for him. It was Finbar, Kip's second-in-command. Walking on two legs and covered in white fur, Finbar was half-human, half-arctic wolf.

'Welcome back,' said Finbar.

Kip couldn't help noticing that he sounded stressed. 'Is the wormhole opening already?' he asked, looking out the giant windows into space.

Space Scouts used wormholes to travel quickly between different galaxies.

'By the time you've downloaded your mission brief, it'll probably be closed,' grumbled MoNa. She was an intelligent starship and could hear everything Kip and Finbar said.

Kip and Finbar exchanged glances. MoNa could be so crabby sometimes! She was busy flying them from the Hoverport into deep space and she hated interruptions when she was concentrating.

The bridge was packed with bleeping gadgets, but best of all was Kip's holographic console. He waved his hand above his head to activate it. It formed a cylinder of blue light around him. Kip hit the button that downloaded his mission brief.

SPACE SCOUT KIP KIRBY MISSION BRIEF

WorldCorp has received friendly communications from the aliens of a planet called Yufe. The aliens request help with developing their technology.

Your mission:

Assist the local aliens and decide if Yufe could be the next Earth.

Awesome! Kip thought. Friendly aliens were always a bonus.

'The wormhole's up ahead,' said Finbar. 'But we don't have much time.'

Kip saw the wormhole, a clump of glowing, electric blue cloud. 'Let's go, Finb—' he began. 'Wait…what's THAT?'

A ginormous rubbery blob, nearly as big as MoNa, was hurtling out of the wormhole. It was heading straight for them.

'Call me crazy, but that looks like the universe's biggest water bomb!' Kip yelled.

CHAPTER 3

Back on Earth, Kip had seen a water bomb in a museum. It was a small balloon that kids used to fill with water and throw at each other for fun. Of course, in the year 2354, no-one on Earth had water to waste.

MoNa's system confirmed it. The blobby object was definitely a water bomb. But it was enormous! And the sub-zero temperatures of deep space had completely frozen the water inside. Now the bomb was full of solid ice!

An ice chunk that big would destroy MoNa if they collided.

'Do something, Kip!' Finbar howled, ears flat against his head. Although Finbar had many wolfish qualities, he was still prone to panicking.

There wasn't time to pilot MoNa out of the way. Kip would have to destroy the water bomb – fast! Desperately, Kip flicked through MoNa's range of guns on his holographic console.

Foam gun… No, that was fun, but only really useful for cleaning dirty starships.

Ray gun…That would explode the ice, but the debris would still smash into MoNa.

The emergency light in the bridge turned red. The giant bomb filled MoNa's windscreen. Finbar covered his eyes with his paws. Kip was almost out of time!

Then suddenly, Kip found just what he needed. MoNa's SunGuns!

A double-barrelled SunGun was mounted on each side of the starship. As soon as Kip stabbed the 'Engage SunGun' button, the bright yellow guns powered up. Kip squinted through the gunsights and aimed at the giant water bomb.

'Cover your ears!' he yelled to Finbar.

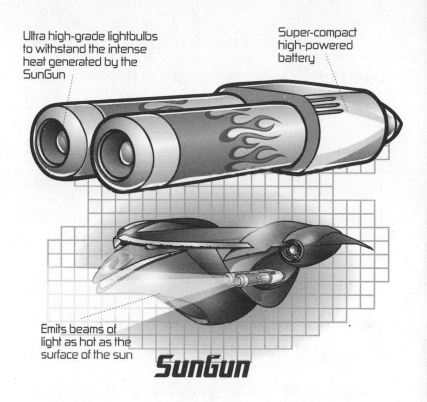

Ultra high-grade lightbulbs to withstand the intense heat generated by the SunGun

Super-compact high-powered battery

Emits beams of light as hot as the surface of the sun

SunGun

Then...

KA-30000M!

The SunGuns fired, and in a nano-second, a wave of 6000-degree heat hit the water bomb.

The water balloon exploded in red, rubbery shreds. Steam hissed everywhere. The SunGuns had melted the ice on impact. The water inside was now boiling hot!

There was a roar as millions of litres of boiling water slammed into MoNa. For a moment, the world went white.

The full force of all that boiling water sent MoNa plunging off-course. Away from the wormhole!

At once, Kip grabbed the controls and switched them from auto-pilot mode. Bashing his holographic steering controls, Kip spun MoNa back towards the wormhole.

'It's about to close!' yelled Finbar.

The swirling clouds were getting thinner and thinner. The wormhole had shrunk to practically nothing.

'We'll make it!' said Kip.

With a determined stomp of his space boot, Kip engaged warp speed. MoNa jumped forwards so fast that he almost lost his lunch of powdered pepperoni pizza.

The wormhole sucked them inside like a vacuum cleaner. Kip piloted MoNa safely through until they popped out the other side, where everything was calm.

Kip wiped his sweaty face with the sleeve of his spacesuit. *Phew,* he thought to himself. *Made it*.

Ahead of them lay the planet Yufe.

Comets streaked across the sky around MoNa. Kip wasn't worried, though. He switched MoNa back to auto-pilot. Her hazard perception systems would detect and avoid the comets.

Kip and Finbar went down to the landing bay. There, MoNa would transport their particles to the surface of Yufe using her Scrambler Beams.

The beams worked by splitting their bodies into tiny particles, sending these through space, and putting them back together on the surface of Yufe.

As Kip ran, his mind ticked over.

Did the aliens on Yufe send that water bomb into space? If they did, there must be a lot of water on their planet. That could mean it had Earth-like conditions.

But why would the aliens be throwing water bombs through wormholes? thought Kip. *Either that was an accident, or they're not as friendly as they seemed!*

CHAPTER 4

Kip and Finbar's particles whizzed through space and reformed on the surface of Yufe.

When Kip was in one piece again, he looked around and noticed it was early in the evening. Above them comets shot past, more common than stars in the Earth sky. And although it was getting dark, Yufe hummed with life. Everywhere Kip looked, he saw alien kids running around, but not a single grown-up.

Those kids look about my age! Kip thought. *Shouldn't they be home having dinner?*

The other thing that struck Kip was how much the kids of Yufe looked like him. They wore sporty shorts and T-shirts, just like Kip did at home. They walked like him, talked like him…they even rode hoverboards like him!

The big difference was that these kids had bright green skin and three eyes waving on long stalks on top of their heads.

Kip checked his SpaceCuff's Air Analyser. He wasn't surprised that the air on Yufe was safe for humans to breathe.

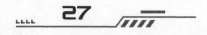

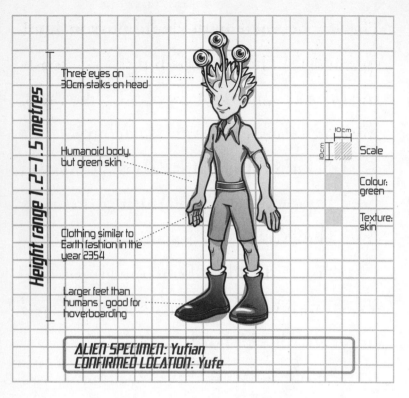

Height range 1.2-1.5 metres

Three eyes on 30cm stalks on head

Humanoid body, but green skin

Clothing similar to Earth fashion in the year 2354

Larger feet than humans - good for hoverboarding

10cm

10cm

Scale

Colour: green

Texture: skin

ALIEN SPECIMEN: Yufian
CONFIRMED LOCATION: Yufe

In fact, when Kip took off his helmet and had a good look around, he saw Yufe was a lot like Earth in other ways too.

Kip and Finbar were standing on a busy city street, lined with massive skyscrapers.

The sky teemed with single-person light spacecraft. There were buildings, roads and even a fountain nearby — just like there were in cities on Earth. Of course, not everything was the same. When Kip looked through a gap between two buildings, he saw a field full of awesome-looking rides.

He turned to Finbar, who was looking more closely at the fountain. Kip guessed he was hoping to find water.

'Either the water here is brown and sludgy,' said Finbar, 'or that fountain's full of melted chocolate.'

Kip analysed the brown liquid with his SpaceCuff. Finbar was right! It was chocolate. And judging by the way kids

were swarming all around, it was free to drink from any time. Kip took off his space glove and stuck his finger in the fountain.

A planet where chocolate's free any time? he thought. *That's awes—*

WHOOSH!

A three-eyed kid on a hoverboard whizzed past Kip's head. The edge of the board clipped Finbar's ear. But the kid didn't even stop to say sorry.

Finbar growled and rubbed his ear. Kip was sorry Finbar was hurt, but he also felt excited. He couldn't believe how many kids on hoverboards there were.

On Earth, hoverboarders were only allowed in special mid-air skate bowls.

Grown-ups found them a nuisance on the streets. Kip broke the rules whenever he could, but it didn't even look like there were rules here.

'The more I see of Yufe, the more I like it!' Kip said. This place was perfect for Earth 2.

Finbar pursed his lips. He was more cautious than Kip.

'That must be where the water bomb came from,' Finbar said. He pointed at the top of a distant hill, where some kids were messing around with a silver machine.

'It's an ultra-long-range cannon,' Finbar continued, eyeing the machine's powerful gun barrel.

'Somehow I don't think it's meant for firing water bombs,' Kip said. The machine looked just like Earth's anti-comet cannons.

They watched as the kids launched a huge green water bomb into space. This one nearly took out a low-flying satellite! The kids clearly had no idea how to fire the cannon properly.

'Our water bomb was way bigger than that,' said Kip. 'Maybe it came from somewhere else.'

'Irresponsible, anyway,' Finbar sniffed.

Kip gave him a friendly punch on the arm. 'But fun!' he replied.

Finbar rolled his eyes towards the sky. Then he stopped. 'Kip, look at that comet!

It's much bigger than all the others.'

Kip glanced up. Finbar was right, but so what? There were all kinds of comets flying around this planet. Kip wasn't going to let Finbar put him off Yufe.

'My wolf senses tell me something's weird about that comet,' Finbar went on, his fur bristling.

Before Kip could tell Finbar he was overreacting, they were interrupted.

'Welcome to Yufe,' said a voice. It sounded just like Kip's.

Kip and Finbar turned around to see an alien kid, exactly Kip's height. His three brown eyes were the same colour as Kip's. He wore a red T-shirt that was just like

one Kip had at home. In fact, apart from his green skin and three eye stalks, he was a lot like Kip.

'Er…hi,' Kip answered, stunned that this alien kid even spoke his language.

Towering over the kid was what looked like a cross between a wolf and an alien being. He was furry all over. He looked a lot like Finbar, except his fur was black, not white.

A creepy, excited shiver ran up Kip's spine. *I think we've just met our alien doubles!* he thought.

'This is Fergus, and I'm Ker,' said the kid. His three eyes twitched first left, then right. Kip noticed his middle eye stalk was

longer than the others.

'Ker's the leader of Yufe,' Fergus added firmly.

A kid in charge of an entire planet? Kip couldn't believe it.

Kip noticed Fergus giving Finbar a yellow-eyed stare, as if daring him to disagree.

Kip had a bad feeling about Fergus. Something about that alien wolf seemed like trouble.

CHAPTER 5

Kip and Finbar smiled uncertainly at Ker and Fergus. It was pretty freaky meeting an alien version of yourself deep in an unexplored galaxy, but Kip still thought Yufe was fun.

'Come on,' said Ker. 'I'll show you around. My place is over there.'

Like Kip, Ker lived in an apartment

building. Kip and his parents lived in a tiny apartment thousands of storeys up. But Ker seemed to have this apartment building all to himself. And it was awesome!

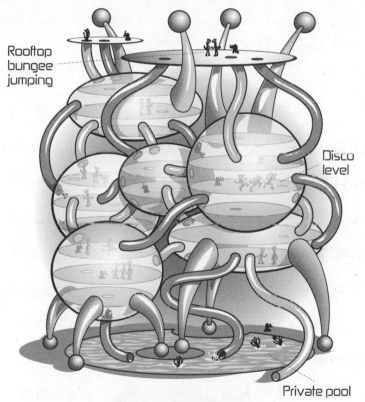

Rooftop bungee jumping

Disco level

Private pool

Ker's House

There was no lift between the floors. Instead, transparent chutes sucked you up the outside of the building, and slides ran from the top floor to the ground. At the bottom of the building was a swimming pool and garden.

Heaps of Ker's friends were relaxing on motorised lilos as Refresherbots brought them food and drinks.

Then Kip spotted something sailing through the air towards his head. It looked a bit like a chocolate éclair, except the icing was orange and the cream inside was frothing.

'Food fight!' yelled one of Ker's friends.

Ker whipped a portable mini-laser

from his pocket and blasted the alien éclair to pieces. He laughed as cream splattered everywhere.

'There's nothing this cool on Earth!' Kip said to Finbar.

'Or this messy,' Finbar muttered, picking blue baked beans out of his fur. 'Shouldn't Ker be more responsible?' He's supposed to be running this planet!'

But Kip was too caught up in the food fight to listen. His SpaceCuff was buzzing, but he ignored that too.

He grabbed a hamburger-shaped melon from a passing Refresherbot and lobbed it at an alien kid.

SPLAT!

'I'm going to get you, Alien Boy!' the kid shrieked at Kip.

Kip was swept into the game. Finbar hated getting his white fur dirty, so he ducked behind a tree.

Kip hurled a green ice-cream sundae into the air. It sailed into the street, smashing into a lone figure. The kid was wearing a long black cloak instead of bright colours like the rest of the kids.

'Hey, sorry,' called Finbar, as Kip ran off. 'Kip didn't mean to hit you.'

The kid didn't seem to have noticed the ice-cream, though. Instead, he was staring anxiously towards the large comet in the sky. But at the sound of Finbar's voice, the kid vanished down a narrow alley behind Ker's apartment building.

The food fight had turned into a bombing competition in the pool. Ker and Kip were relaxing on deckchairs, green drinks bubbling over the top of their glasses. Fergus sat by Ker's side.

'Who was that kid wearing the black cloak?' Finbar asked, coming over.

'Probably your stupid sist—' Fergus began, muttering under his breath.

'Oh, who cares, Fergus,' said Ker, grinning at Kip. 'Fergus worries about details, but I just like to have fun. That's what makes me a popular leader.'

'And why Yufe is obviously the best

planet EVER!' Kip said. 'In fact…'

Kip decided that now was the perfect time to explain his mission to Ker. As leader of Yufe, Ker could surely authorise Earth's people to move in. To Kip, this planet looked perfect. Clean air. Water to spare. And non-stop fun all day!

After telling Ker about Earth's situation, Kip asked the big question. 'Could we bring some people here to live? Some more kids and their mums and dads?'

A puzzled expression crossed Ker's face. 'Kids? Mumsandads? What are they?' he asked.

Now Kip was confused. 'Kids are like us. Mums and dads are wrinkled old people. They make rules and talk about eating your vegies a lot. Oh, and they love telling corny jokes.'

Ker made a fake spewing noise. 'Mumsandads sound awful!'

Obviously, Ker didn't know grown-ups even existed. It explained why the kids were running riot on Yufe. The planet was kids only!

But if all they do is have fun, how did kids manage to invent the cool stuff they've got here? Kip wondered.

Finbar had questions of his own. 'How are new kids born without grown-ups?' he asked.

Ker explained that no-one on Yufe was

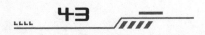

older than 12. Just before kids turned 13, they started aging in reverse until they were toddlers. No-one died or was born — kids just got older and younger over and over again.

Kip was stunned. With no grown-ups, life would be paradise. No school, no bedtime and no-one telling you what to do!

'Well, you're welcome to move here, Kip,' Ker said. 'As long as you like to have fun!'

Fergus gave a low growl. 'Ker's in charge, though – don't forget.'

Kip smiled. Even if Fergus was a bit unfriendly, Ker's offer was tempting. *Very* tempting.

'There's just one condition,' Ker added. 'You've got to leave all those horrible mumsandads behind!'

CHAPTER 6

Space Scouting was full of big decisions. But this was one of the toughest Kip had ever faced. If he could convince WorldCorp that Yufe was Earth 2, then Earth's kids would be guaranteed a life of never-ending fun.

Plus I'd get all the glory as the Scout who discovered the next Earth! Kip thought.

But with a twinge he remembered his dad's jokes. Although he might be silly sometimes, his dad was still loveable.

Could I really move to a new galaxy and leave my parents behind? he wondered.

Kip was so deep in thought, he hardly noticed his SpaceCuff buzzing furiously.

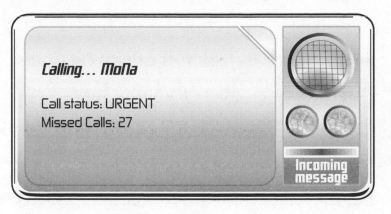

Calling... MoNa

Call status: URGENT
Missed Calls: 27

Incoming message

'Where have you been?' squawked MoNa when Kip took the call. But strangely, she didn't sound furious.

She just sounds… panicked, thought Kip. He felt a prickle of fear in his stomach.

'My system detected a large comet near Yufe before you landed,' MoNa continued. 'Now my sensors are telling me it's gone rogue!'

Oh no! A rogue comet was one that'd broken its orbit. It would cause catastrophic damage if it crashed into a planet.

'That big comet we saw,' Finbar said gravely. 'I knew there was something wrong with it!'

Kip turned to Ker. He couldn't believe the look on Ker's face. He was *grinning*. It was as if Ker hadn't heard what Finbar said.

'Want to go and muck around on the

360-degree waterslide?' Ker asked.

'You're kidding, right?' Kip answered. 'Your planet is facing a massive crisis, and—'

'Crisis?' echoed Ker. 'What's a crisis?'

Kip shook his head. The kids on Yufe were used to having fun all the time. They were totally unprepared for danger!

'Who are the smartest kids on Yufe?' Kip asked Ker. 'We're going to need everyone's help to solve this.'

Ker shrugged. 'Why worry so much when you could be having fun?' he said. 'It'll work itself out.'

Kip took one look at Finbar and knew what he was thinking. For the leader of a planet, Ker had no idea how to run things.

'Do you think any of the other kids would take us seriously?' Finbar whispered.

Kip thought it was worth a shot. Telling Ker they were going to have a better look around, he and Finbar left.

Outside, there were kids everywhere.

'Find the 12-year-olds. They're probably the smartest!' Kip said.

Finbar nodded and they took off into the crowd. Kip ran up to a girl who looked about his age.

'Excuse me,' he said. 'Your planet is in grave danger and we need your help.'

The girl's eyes twitched. For a second, Kip felt hopeful.

Then…

'You're it!' the girl yelled, running off.

Kip's shoulders slumped. The kids were in the middle of a chasey game. They'd be impossible to distract now!

Finbar chased after a boy wearing a peaked silver cap. Running up behind him, Finbar reached out a paw. But then the kid vanished! His silver cap fluttered to the ground.

'Must be an Exploding Matter Cap!' Kip panted, running up to Finbar.

Exploding Matter Caps used the same technology as Scrambler Beams. Electrodes inside the cap blew your particles so wide apart that you turned invisible temporarily. The effect wore off in two minutes or so, when your particles flew back together. *Excellent fun for chasey*, Kip thought darkly. *But downright annoying when you've got a planet to save!*

'After him!' Finbar yelled as another lanky kid ran by in an Exploding Matter Cap.

Kip sped after the kid and made a grab at him. Too late! The kid disappeared, leaving Kip holding an empty cap.

'DON'T YOU REALISE THIS ISN'T A GAME?' Kip yelled.

With no grown-ups to ask for help, Kip and Finbar were on their own.

'We could call MoNa and ask her to send two Scramblers,' Finbar said quietly.

Fashionable and durable
titanium-cotton blend

Eye-stalk holes
in peak of cap

'At least *we* could escape that way.'

Kip shook his head grimly. It wouldn't
be honourable for a Space Scout to escape
and leave a planet in danger.

Somehow he had to convince a planet of fun-loving kids that their fun would soon be over unless they helped him.

Either that, or stop the rogue comet single-handedly.

And both options seemed impossible!

CHAPTER 7

There has to be a way out of this mess, Kip thought, his teeth gritted.

Hoping an idea would come to him, Kip scanned the fun-filled city.

Kids in Exploding Matter Caps. The chocolate fountain. The cannon they'd seen when they first landed.

It's all very high-tech gear for a society

of kids who do nothing but have fun, thought Kip.

'Who invented this stuff, Finbar?' asked Kip.

As he said it, a figure in a black cloak hurried along the alley near Ker's house, catching Kip's eye.

Kip turned to Finbar. 'Did you just see that kid in the cloak?' he asked.

'Yes,' said Finbar. 'I saw another kid dressed the same earlier on.'

A theory was forming in Kip's mind. A high tech city full of cool inventions. Mysterious kids in cloaks. Plus, didn't WorldCorp say someone had been communicating with them, wanting help with technology? That didn't sound like Ker!

'Ker and the fun-loving kids can't be the only ones living on Yufe!' Kip said in a low voice.

Finbar nodded. 'I hope you're right.'

'Those cloaked kids might be able to help us,' Kip went on. 'If we can find them.'

For the millionth time since he became a Space Scout, Kip was grateful for Finbar's wolf side. His 2iC raced to the alley and sniffed the ground expertly. Within moments, his tail began wagging.

'I've picked up the kid's scent,' Finbar said. 'Now all we have to do is follow it.'

Stealth was critical. For whatever reason, the cloaked kids were keeping to themselves. Kip had to find their hide-out and figure out a way to talk to them before they saw him and ran off.

Kip set his brand-new Ace-teroid space boots to silent by adjusting a dial on the ankle. At once, a spongy balloon shot out of the heel, filling with gel and enveloping the entire boot in a soft, squishy cover. No matter what surface Kip walked on, his footsteps wouldn't make a sound.

Finbar took his boots off completely and stashed them in his backpack. He padded along silently on his soft paws.

Finbar led the way. His nose was pointed to the ground, sniffing hard. Behind him, Kip stuck to the shadows, the way he'd learnt in Space Scout stealth training.

The dark alley twisted and turned, leading Kip and Finbar away from Ker's apartment building.

'Are you sure this is right?' asked Kip.

Finbar nodded. 'The scent's getting stronger,' he said.

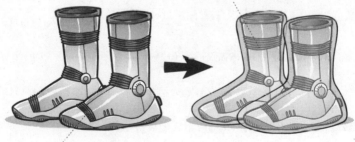

Pierce-proof polymer fills with noise-cancelling hydrogel for stealth

Sleek and stylish, fits to wearer's foot

Ace-teroid Space Boots

He followed it until they came to a black metal trapdoor that was cut into the road. It was almost invisible. Kneeling down, Kip slowly levered up the door.

'What if they're hostile?' Finbar whispered in a worried tone.

Without answering, Kip wriggled through the trapdoor. He didn't know what would be waiting on the other side, but he had a feeling these kids were their best hope for saving Yufe.

Kip found himself in a dark tunnel. A dull light shone further along, so Kip crept towards it. Finbar followed close behind.

The light was coming from a room ahead. The door had been left slightly ajar.

Kip pushed on it gently.

CRRRR-EEEEEAK!

The door slowly swung open.

Kip sucked in a gasp. Inside the room was a massive laboratory filled with hundreds of kids in black cloaks!

Every inch of the lab was packed with gadgets. There were blinking computer screens, bleeping monitors and silver machines Kip couldn't identify. Kids in cloaks were busy scribbling notes and consulting clipboards.

'Err...excuse me,' said Kip in his loudest voice.

The kids all turned to look, and the room fell silent.

'I'm Kip and this is Finbar,' Kip said to the kids. 'We're from planet Earth. We've come about the rogue comet. Your planet is in serious danger.'

A girl exactly Kip's height stepped forward. Kip noticed her skin was pasty and pale green instead of bright green like the kids on the surface.

'We know,' said the alien girl, her three eye-stalks fixing on Kip.

There was something oddly familiar about the way the middle eye was longer than the others...

'We feared that comet might go rogue,' the girl said. 'We called Earth to ask for help. We thought you were here to help us!

But then you just wanted to have fun, like Ker and all the rest. We had to get on with solving things ourselves.'

Kip felt sheepish. 'I'm sorry about that. But who are you?' he asked. 'And more importantly, how are we going to save Yufe?'

CHAPTER 8

The tall, pale-skinned alien girl studied Kip carefully. Then she seemed to decide to trust him. Her suspicious look faded.

'We call ourselves the Undergrounders,' she said. 'I'm Kal, the leader.'

Kal explained that, like Ker and the others, the Undergrounders never grew

older than 12. But unlike the kids who lived on the surface, the Undergrounders knew that some things had to be taken seriously.

'This galaxy's full of big comets,' Kal explained. 'It was only a matter of time before one crashed into us.'

'I suppose Ker and the others didn't want to worry about comets spoiling their fun,' Finbar said.

'That's right. And over time, it became easier to shut ourselves off and live down here,' Kal continued, nodding. 'We worked on protecting Yufe in case of a crisis.'

'Did you also invent all the high-tech gadgets on Yufe?' asked Kip, thinking of the chocolate fountain and hoverboards.

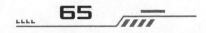

'Of course we did,' said Kal. 'My team don't only invent serious stuff. We invent all of Yufe's fun gadgets here too.'

Kip had lots of questions to ask, but one of the kids at a computer screen suddenly spun around on his chair.

'By my calculations, we've only got 7 minutes and 16 seconds 'til the comet enters our atmosphere!' the kid said urgently.

Kal's skin turned an even more sickly shade of green. 'Once the comet enters our atmosphere, we can't stop it,' she said helplessly. 'We thought we had the perfect defence against rogue comets.'

Kip remembered something. *Does she*

mean the machine those kids were using to fire water bombs?

'Your cannon?' Kip guessed aloud. 'That thing could blast a rogue comet to smithereens!'

'That was our plan,' Kal agreed. 'We've been working on the Destroyer for months.'

The nearby Undergrounders fell silent. A pinkish blush crept over their green cheeks.

'But there's something wrong with it,' Kal admitted. 'We can't get it to fire straight. Our best kids are working on it but getting nowhere.'

Hope flickered in Kip's chest. 'Finbar's got incredible wolf vision,' he said.

'And I topped Weapon Maintenance back in Space Scout training.'

'Between us, we might be able to help,' Finbar agreed.

The Undergrounders leapt to their feet. Together with Kip and Finbar, they raced to the surface.

Outside, the surface kids were playing as much as ever. Kip thought he spotted Ker swimming in the chocolate fountain.

No-one was looking at the rogue comet, which looked even huger in the sky. Kip could see a red tail blazing behind it. The surface kids didn't seem to notice that it was headed straight for them!

Kip and the Undergrounders ran to

the cannon on top of the hill. The area was deserted. Shredded water balloons lay all over the ground.

'We made it exactly the same as Earth's anti-comet cannons,' Kal explained. 'WorldCorp provided the design. We have a missile to fire at the comet when we're ready. But the surface kids have been mucking around with water bombs, so we've hardly had time to practise. Our water expands and the other kids think it's hilarious.'

'Your water expands? That's amazing!' exclaimed Kip. 'So *that's* why the water bomb that came through the wormhole was so enormous!'

200 x zoom
gunsight

Fires anti-comet
grade missiles

The Destroyer – Anti-comet Cannon

'In any case, none of us can get the aim right,' Kal said.

Finbar squinted at the gunsight. 'Nothing wrong that I can see,' he said.

Kip looked into the gunsight too. With a simple turn of the cannon on its rotating base, he lined up the comet immediately. Someone loaded a missile into the machine. The target seemed impossible to miss.

So what's going wrong? he thought, staring around at the Undergrounders as he tried to crack the problem.

The Undergrounders stared back at him, their three eyes wide with tension.

Wait…three eyes…

The Undergrounders had copied the design of cannons on Earth. Cannons that were designed to be fired by people with *two* eyes. With three eyes, the aliens couldn't aim straight! Kip explained his

theory to the Undergrounders.

Kal slapped a hand to her forehead. 'Of course!'

'I've got two eyes. Plus, I've been trained to fire all kinds of weapons,' Kip said. 'Do you want me to fire the cannon for you?'

Kal nodded. 'You'd better hurry,' she said quickly.

'Right,' said Kip. 'Load the missile.'

Kal and the Undergrounders loaded a huge missile into the cannon.

'Now, keep the surface kids away from here,' said Kip. 'The last thing we need is a hoverboard crashing into the cannon.'

Kip positioned himself in front of the

gunsight. His finger, trembling slightly, rested on the trigger.

He was just about to fire when a voice behind him broke his concentration.

'What do you think you're doing, Earthling?' Fergus growled. 'You think you can just come here and start ordering us around?'

CHAPTER 9

Anger boiled inside Kip. Every second wasted brought Yufe closer to danger!

'We're saving your planet,' Kip said shortly. 'Otherwise, that comet will crush you all!'

Fergus's eyes glittered. 'You and your wolf can't come here acting like you're in charge,' he growled.

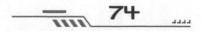

So this is what Ker meant when he said Fergus looks after the details, Kip thought angrily. *Ker has fun and stays popular — while Fergus makes sure no-one's threatening his leadership!*

'I'M TRYING TO HELP YOU!' Kip exploded.

'You're trying to steal Ker's leadership and so's Kal,' Fergus snapped. 'We don't need your help. Ker's the leader around here, and I'm the alpha wolf.'

'Wolves are pack animals,' Finbar whispered. 'Fergus thinks we're acting out of turn, because he's the wolf in charge.'

'Whatever.' Kip rolled his eyes. This was no time for wolf politics. He had to blast that comet.

But Fergus snarled at Finbar. He was definitely picking a fight!

'Sixty seconds to stop it!' shrieked one of the Undergrounders.

The comet still looked a way off, but it was moving super fast.

Fergus circled Finbar, teeth bared. He was about to attack! But Finbar stood his ground.

Fergus lunged!

Finbar grabbed Fergus firmly by the shoulders, making him squeak in surprise. It looked very strange, like the two wolves were dancing.

Finbar locked eyes with Fergus. He stared hard. Then suddenly…

Fergus whimpered and dropped to his knees.

'Thirty seconds!' yelled the kids.

Kip swung back to the Destroyer. He got the comet in his sights and fired!

The missile hurtled through the sky towards the comet, then…

KA-3OOOOM!

There was a flash of white. A moment later, debris from the exploded comet rained down on them.

The missile had hit the comet dead-centre. Yufe was saved!

At the sound of the crash, the surface kids came running towards the Destroyer. Ker led the way. For once, he wasn't grinning.

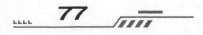

'That was a really close one!' he said to Kal, surprised. He even looked a little sheepish. 'I'm sorry I didn't believe you about the comet. I thought you were trying to stop my fun. And Fergus said you wanted the leadership.'

Kal turned to Kip. 'Our older sister was leader – but when she grew young again, someone had to take over. Ker and I are twins, so we didn't know who it should be.'

Twins! thought Kip. *No wonder they're alike...*

'Seems like Ker got all the good-time genes and you got the serious ones,' Kip answered.

'The kids wanted Ker as leader,' Kal said. 'He's more fun than me.'

Ker looked at his feet. 'I liked being popular,' he admitted. 'But I can see a leader needs to be fun *and* serious sometimes too. Maybe Kal and I could lead together.'

'You'd have to agree to open some schools so we can learn,' Kal said.

'Will we have to go every day?' Ker asked, horrified.

'Of course not,' said Kal. 'Only on weekdays.'

Obviously it was going to take the two groups of kids a while to get used to each other again.

Reluctantly, Kip had to admit Yufe

was not Earth 2. He couldn't imagine WorldCorp letting only kids move to a new planet. He wasn't even sure it was a good idea himself! But least he'd helped the kids on Yufe by blasting away the comet.

'Come on, Finbar,' said Kip. 'It's time to get going.'

But before Kip could call MoNa, he heard a familiar growl right behind him.

Fergus again! Except he didn't attack. He sat next to Finbar, wagging his tail.

'Can I come with you?' he asked.

'Why is he being so nice?' Kip whispered to Finbar. 'What did you do to him?'

'I just stared him down,' said Finbar. 'And now he thinks *I'm* the alpha wolf.

The only problem is, now he'll want to stay with us.'

Kip grinned. 'WorldCorp's Gadget Design people sent me this yak-flavoured squeaky ball,' he said, pulling it from his backpack.

Finbar raised his fuzzy eyebrows.

'It's motion-sensor activated,' Kip explained. 'As soon as you catch it, the ball bounces off in another direction. It's a game of fetch that never ends! It's supposed to keep you fit on long space flights.'

Kip told Finbar to look away while he threw the ball. The ball was irresistible to wolves and Kip wanted it to work on Fergus, not Finbar.

Kip hurled the ball. Fergus's black ears pricked up and he bounded off after it.

That should keep him happy for a while! Kip thought with a grin.

CHAPTER 10

Fergus reached the ball in a few powerful strides. His mouth closed around it, savouring the yak flavour. Then the ball flew out of his mouth and sped off in the opposite direction.

For a second, Fergus looked stunned. Then he raced after the ball again.

As soon as he saw his plan was working,

Kip called MoNa.

'I thought you were never going to explode that comet,' MoNa grumbled.

Ker overheard MoNa's loud voice through Kip's SpaceCuff. 'Is that one of those mumsandads?' Ker asked, horrified.

'Er…no,' Kip said. 'That's my bossy starship. Mums and dads are normally nicer than that.'

Ker looked doubtful. Kip could tell he seriously wasn't ready to let grown-ups move to Yufe.

Two Scrambler Beams shot down from MoNa, who was hovering just beyond Yufe's atmosphere. Ker held out his hand for a goodbye handshake.

As Kip shook Ker's hand, he thought about how similar they were. Both were responsible for helping to keep their people safe. Ker spent most of his time having fun – and Kip knew that was important, but hard work was necessary too.

Next, Kip and Finbar said goodbye to Kal and the Undergrounders.

'As soon as I get home, I'll send you an update on all of Earth's new technology via intergalactic satellite phone,' Kip promised.

The Undergrounders whispered excitedly. Their love of tech was on the geeky side. Kip hoped they'd learn to have fun too.

Before leaving, Kip filled his drink bottle from a nearby chocolate fountain. The bottle was computerised, so Kip could program in the temperature he wanted his drink. The bottle also had the latest Pumpastraw feature, so the drink pumped into Kip's mouth automatically.

Kal gave him a second bottle filled with water from Yufe. 'Here's a sample for you,' she said. 'Maybe your scientists can work out how to make the water on Earth expand too.'

'Thanks,' said Kip, as he stepped into his Scrambler. Finbar did the same.

Seconds later, their particles had been scrambled and beamed through space.

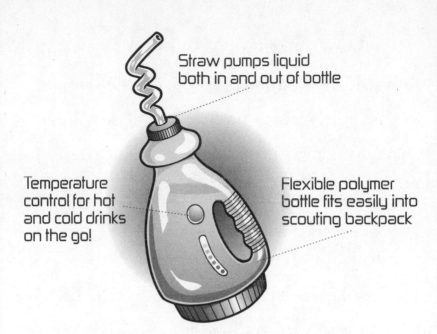

Straw pumps liquid
both in and out of bottle

Temperature
control for hot
and cold drinks
on the go!

Flexible polymer
bottle fits easily into
scouting backpack

They were back on board MoNa.

Kip was exhausted. But there was one
more thing to do. His mission report!

Together, he and Finbar made their way
to the bridge.

Kip sat on his captain's chair, engaged
his holographic console and began to type.

CAPTAIN'S LOG
Yufe

Climate: Almost identical to Earth 1.

Population: Three-eyed green alien kids who never grow older than 12. The kids are split into two groups – the technology-loving Undergrounders and the fun-loving kids on the surface.

Highlights: Chocolate fountains and freedom to hoverboard anywhere.

Water that expands in cold temperatures. Could help with Earth's water shortages.

Lowlights: Although Yufe is great fun, the surface kids are unprepared for any kind of crisis.

Recommendation: Yufe is a kids-only planet, which means it cannot be Earth 2. Anyway, after observing conditions on Yufe, I now realise grown-ups are useful sometimes. Running an entire planet is a huge responsibility!

KIP KIRBY, SPACE SCOUT #50

Relieved, Kip hit send. His tasks were complete, for this mission at least.

He scrolled to the holophone function on his console and punched in Jett's number. He couldn't wait to find out how the rest of the moon camping trip went.

When Jett answered the call, it wasn't just his voice or picture that came through. Instead, a three-dimensional holographic version of Jett was beamed from the console into MoNa's bridge.

Jett's hologram sat down next to Kip and put its holographic feet up on the dash.

'Your dad was pretty mad about the Space Stream at first,' holographic Jett said.

Kip winced.

'But once it came back from the Hoverport, he calmed down.'

Relief washed over Kip.

'Your dad *did* tell terrible jokes all the way home,' Jett said, grinning.

Kip put his head in his hands. Why did grown-ups have to be so embarrassing?

'Hey, how do you know Saturn's married?' Jett asked.

Kip groaned. This was one of his dad's favourite and most terrible jokes! 'Because it wears rings,' he said, laughing despite himself.

Holographic Jett turned to Kip with a big smile on his face. 'I've just had a great idea!' he said. 'Maybe our next camping trip should be kids-only.'

Kip paused, remembering everything that had happened on Yufe.

'Er…kids-only?' he said. 'I'll need to think about that!'

THE END